Odeum Spotlights

Olly Todd

The Earthquake and the Quail

You're like an earthquake I met once.
He was shaking DVD shelves to the floor at a party
When I bumped into him. You should have seen the snarl
On his face when he turned around, felt the depth of his breathing.
The shelves were just the beginning though.
He said he wanted to learn how to tear roads apart,
Send lost dogs straight to hell for the anguish they cause.
There aren't that many lost dogs around here
But there is one motley pack that riles him
For their refusal to go back to their families.
Can't they read the lost dog flyers said the earthquake.
One night he watched a young man moving in with his girlfriend.
He only had a couple of bags and what looked like a typewriter.
They ordered pizza and chicken wings.
When the young man answered the front-garden gate
To the delivery boy, paid and returned with the food,
He hadn't even considered the latch.
His girlfriend hadn't warned him about the latch.
Wow I didn't realise earthquakes could be so omnipresent I said.
Oh yeah, you just gotta come up to the surface now and again.
Isn't that difficult without causing a rumble,
How do you remain inconspicuous?
I meditate said the earthquake, cleanse the mind,
When I'm in the zone I could close my fist around a quail's egg,
Keep a pocketful of sugarwork in tact mate.

Walking Around Money

Having reimagined the allotments
As battlefields a hundred times
With marine ply swords and locust trees,
Bubbling brooks laced with conker bombs
And with the hard-won Mirehouse reservoir
An audible burden like culture for Mancs—

Post punk is internal but a costume nonetheless—
It was time for fashion, fitting in,
The discontent of the three-day week
The tedium of civil war men,
Weetabix sandwiches, sugar, Bowie's quiet,
My own Zen scholarship zeroed in on

Yellow masonite, sapiently drilling
From the hillbrow's old pipes runny
Honey for bait for splake—I had fished
In the days during woodland war when,
Cloacally emplaced like arsenic again
I had defied the harbour master.

For my next phase I had phrases planned.
Here's some walking around money.
Cast No Shadow on the Dolphin jukebox.
Trapped in dreamt drilling, gutlessly upbeat,
Wanted, bitten in the draughty stables, knowing
You're a gonner but caring for your exit.

NX RD

I.
Dinner earlier at the team cantina Argentina
Was good although the starters trumped the mains as per.
The Transworld article *Waterloo to Anywhere*
Was a let down too, omitting, as it apparently did,
My tennis court grind. I beat furs and fold throws,
Listen to the heartbreak guys, only one of whom is yet
To lace the boots that would better will his drowning.
Next I go for Bonnie's *Angel From Montgomery,*
Fork old tuna from the ramekin.

II.
I walked Kennington tonight wondering whose
Whistle to jinx. I'm stig, immer durstig, altruistic.
That Lennon song on the labour tape was true.
I'm still to wire the speakers from lounge to kitchen like home
But the Bluetooth carries well.
Ah nightcap city, rattley rocks.
It had been a time to skid a mile in life's-a-beach shoes; itch
In Fresno denim, go Cajun, load the jukebox and circle the Marquis bar.
New Cross from the perspective where no student is ugly anymore.

III.
Not even the green hairs who hit the loos in threes.
We loved it when that actor would smoke, would smoke
Away wholesome America like a cist burial. When he smokes
And stamps his feet into the truckstop snow having locked
His lighter in the rattletrap cab our lilliputian urge to bruise him
Subsides as if we'd steadied the bore through a brittle thing.
We compared pre credit crunch Belgravia free booze parties,
Baseball stadium parties in Echo Park—pulled meats
And pomegranate barbecued on car bumpers.

Repose on the Flight into Egypt

How lonely to be awed by people,
Find them funny or sexy.
To find a person funny or sexy is absurd.
The nival cadenza, calocarpa, scarlet moss,
The only red life in their unending white landscape.
How can we be so impressed, as sparkling duly viewing these
Or oystercatchers
Or northern lights
That we should laugh at a person or let go?
Even naked and quizzical, at their best,
Still there shouldn't be power possessed as to stun.
In odeum spotlights they are merely small.
In traffic they are just skin.
To be gone into by someone though, rephrased in their laughter
Is to sit up hip to hip in the soul's odeon,
Is to have a stranger's hand guide you gently clear in a club,
Accepting profoundly their apology.

Summer at Ladlands

Our love is wallside in a Gluck frame and the white flowers have gone over
Our brinkman mimesis of entrapment works despite literal glass to press against
The forefinger of the pointing hand that shapes your redoubt shakes as if in field glasses
Now what I see when I look at your building is the pareidolia hand of buoyant love
Each domestic room has an equivalent in our faculties, your language-broad lounge
The might of the meat falling from the blue walls, something of the hill town child
Fading against the banisters in the higher altitudes of the upper staircases

The Good Listener

A group of friends is a confessional
That makes of the booth a marked-out field
With linesmen, Bovril boys and mascots
In position over the penitent.

One that has begun to mimic mannerisms
As opposed to speech as the individual learns
To singularise the gang osmosis of influence.
Until closing the posse jostles

On a shryving stool we wish were empty,
Doling out unwelcome Hail Marys like travel sweets.
Until closing the posse jostles, eavesdrops,
Bays, behoves itself to balance and balance judgement.

In a conceit u-turn by way of swapping seats,
We could just as easily be at the mercy of the gallery
Milking roughly and, over by the dip, wooling
Impatiently, late for tupping's advent.

But when were husbandry's brute acts solicited
By the animal other than when it suffers.
Our pounds are down on the pool table.
The Good Listener, open till L8.

The Spiralist

(Watson) has suggested the term 'spiralist' for the socially,
economically and geographically mobile.
– RONALD FRANKENBERG, *Communities in Britain*

Down the blacksmith's the gossip's he's one of those spiralists.
Concerned with the motorcars of visiting sociologists but no car
  of his own, just the wish.
Our oats spiral, broadcast for our lazy pigs.
The runes spiral, hard carved round our Saxon cross.
And the sun, well, it's yet again by Eskdale fell yet we move not.
Gosfer folk is Gosfer folk, that sun now nigh Hardknot.

Fell farmers come down for darts, may bout their boys with lowland
  hands, yet mix they do not.
The yellow insides of a scorpion, torn peaches, could Harrison's new
  'dozer combine them?
Egremont for a matinee, the Bull for a drink, his Bristolian
  sleeplessness welcome at song. We'll fetch him a sunday shirt
  from Whitehaven. Then he'll be gone.

At Greenland Dock

The gilled sift, the billed breathe; both farm the manmade water
But Greenland Dock's sheer walls deny its waterfowl dry land
So Southwark anchors barrel tops to which they drag detritus,
Installed by old cadaver men freelancing extra hours.
Refuse men are sent to scoop out leaves and cans with baskets.
Just shopping baskets soldered to a scaffold pole, perhaps
Homemade despite the public role and badges on their caps.
What had their kit consisted of before this can-do weld
Set smooth their work and increased yield by ten kilos a week?

A little street of leaves pulled from this dredging cage
By a hidden eddy fed the rippling carousel set off
By a great crested grebe. Below the surface her chest had swelled
And then she dove, sensing on the vantablack water the deep shrimp.
I wait for this necklace of leaves to become the arena
Of her re-emergence; the room where she feeds
Her bickering clutch, selects her favourite and with it dives again.
For the water to lose all pattern, for the efferent room to break up,
The abandoned chicks to duck, circle seeing nothing.

Us and Them

Unite the lucky
Commission their oaths
Leave bathtubs beneath chandeliers
Untouched by champagne
Consider filling them with champagne though
Consider quarter-filling them with ash
But stump your rollies in the sand box at South Bank
Hear the music you play
To boost your friends blow away on the wind
Heatscreen Perrier bottles in fading degrees
To mirrors with photos of Marlboros and the Pogues
Steal from the Burberry to give to the Prada

Unite the rich
Commission their oaths
Don't flinch when wealth appears from the heavens
Don't flinch when twenty pound notes
Float onto your upturned palms
Commandeer the hotel rooms of the deserving
The northern and the danced-out
Hang stolen lingerie from the cistern
And give it drunkenly to your girl on her return
To the bedroom modelling the oversized red two piece
In the morning give the lobby staff the slip
And run when your ring tone alerts them

Unite the young
Commission their oaths
Tremble at their sides from knowing
In the alley by the railway station
Tell them the show wouldn't exist without them
Tell them actually it would exist but would be terribly boring
Just you looking at yourself in the mirror all night
Ride your T100 Bonneville, left wrist on your lap
Fingers drumming the benchseat
Head in an openface Bitwell helmet, gunmetal
Scanning Porto di Venezia east and west
For your Broom Scorpio speedboat, wood panelled

Unite the brave
Commission their oaths
Collars-up lean against the wall and smoke
Collars-up lean against the wall, prop one foot
And broodily exhale silver smoke
See your boat in the cruise port and go
Raising the anchor in your mind

Unite the beautiful
Commission their oaths
Hug them and welcome your sweaty friends
The heat in here is turning everyone red
And the guy in green threw up his crab & cranberry canapés
Their sweet aversion to make-up and insistence
On popstud bottoms that collect rainwater, flare and bobble
Only confounds one because where they go they glow
Even in this heat
Deftly it is their midriffs that decorate
Don't dream of asking them to host
Don't dream of asking them to reabsorb the condensation
Their sweat deposits on the sash windows
And heatscreened mirrors that adorn these walls

Tangier Street

I live defiantly on the Dover Road and love that people are going there and that I'm close to them.

Through the binoculars that was weirdly us in the imported brown Camero in the snow.

'Furious'

There was a twelve-count pink eggbox lodged in the white stuff glowing like a polar bear's red gums as the lights changed and the cars lurched; Heidi's fury as colourfully howled.

Call it what you want, toast its resurgence. By Ambleside her coach-trip love goes out anyway and it's just me and her bro until Carlisle.

Alighting that afternoon in Workington I re-read my letters from Lombok & Gili, Nevis & St Kitts.

'Unthinkable'

A seven-mile avenue of rushes and reeds sprang out ahead and flanked brooks that were unthinkable to ford—all the rules and the walls. Toeing bean cans in the water I coveted the swift and blue jay.

I ate Sunblest crusts like a gannet and briskly gained the energy to connect the kiss of feet needed for Harrington's s-bent beach and half-piped harbour.

'Falling'

By now the day's taper guaranteed Lowca's flat roofed silhouette would fall perfectly apart in the spokes of BMXs and the spicy grills of squatted coast home larders.

No brother would prosper in this pebbly life and that's why he returned thank Poseidon, thank St. Christopher.

Three miles to march and if the
wan sun finds a way though Lowca's
letter boxes onto couches, cola cups,
Scaletrix tracks, well I'll wish its
sons a stellar ride, salute their dusty
time trials.

These talc-dry boys always had designs
on my town—my rugged Monte Carlo
—geared up to beat blind our heartful
Jerichoans and industrious St James.

Arriving home, Tangier Street was left
blank for bulb thieves, rope swingers
and worm diggers AKA me, Scouser
and Taff.

'Bravado'

Charged by this rep, we made for
hooking cumuli with pecan tins
from the multi storey roof; two tins
each airing the Solway Firth at its
telepathic ablest.

The Dragonfly of Roquecor

The dragonfly of Roquecor oversees its
Eden dartingly, low above the lavoire.

'The old couple'

M'dame & M'sieur Garonne, old fidel-
istas, garden stiffly in felt hats. They
are unseen, are somewhere in the
coppice, but audible like the spa. What
compliments. You are invisible. You
are heard. It's like water.

'Corps d'état'

How do we infer their politics? By the
cut and colour of their coats, coat-
hooked on the leaning rake?

'Gasping'

They were once the gasping newly-
weds crushed and buried by the horned
half-mountain *Roc du Noblis*.

'All around us'

We become the weeping wedding
party, its best men and bridesmaids,
its travel-weary in-laws. All around us
on the valley wind are the speeches.
The wedding wine and the ceremonial
pighead apple—picked from a tree
planted by the Garonnes—bring the
dragonfly from its hunger grid above
the green water

Desert, Desert, Garden

after a fight in Dudley, sixty-two, sixty-three.'
Don't talk to me about your mojo and the British blues boom.
It's all just facile graffiti. Yes it's surrender, can be scolding
But if gracious, with stillness and calm, gets you the rhine-
Stones and the white fox furs. That's universal. But you, you
Wanted a spike of experience. The energy centre. Inflammable
Power. To be intense and on. The Santa Ana winds. The growth
Of the flower of love. To be blinded by all the brass. Desert, desert,
Garden. You've lived the jazz you grieved for, having dodged
Whatever—a twist of birds in the street trees—to do so but go on then

Do, do live your afternoons through a blurry video of green fields
Filmed on flickery High-8, the date-reel ticking at the bottom
Of the screen, air shots of abbeys and yellow glades in whose winds
You imagine yourself to fly pre-industrially, mantelpiece stone
Of Keats House still firm in its Pennine mountain, the ticking
Round of a pushbike wheel, its spokes brought to taughtness
By sound the Italian way, you are free to assume. All you wished
And whistled for played out, done in down a straight street,
The camera swooping now over a town, watching the wheels.
We don't write our surrenders on some wall in the middle
Of the night and seek their acknowledgement through binoculars
In the morning from some sun-lit emergency exit. I often ask
people about you *'...eventually he was just whistling,*
but he was whistling just great.'